THE UNIQUE HAMLET

A HITHERTO UNCHRONICLED ADVENTURE
OF MR. SHERLOCK HOLMES

THE UNIQUE HAMLET

A HITHERTO UNCHRONICLED ADVENTURE
OF MR. SHERLOCK HOLMES

BY

VINCENT STARRETT

PRIVATELY PRINTED
FOR THE FRIENDS OF WALTER M. HILL
CHICAGO ILLINOIS AT CHRISTMAS
NINETEEN HUNDRED TWENTY

THE ADVENTURE OF THE UNIQUE HAMLET

I

"HOLMES," said I, one morning as I stood in our bay window, looking idly into the street, "surely here comes a madman. Someone has incautiously left the door open and the poor fellow has slipped out. What a pity!"

It was a glorious morning in the spring, with a fresh breeze and inviting sunlight, but as it was rather early few persons were astir. Birds twittered under the neighboring eaves, and from the far end of the thoroughfare came faintly the droning cry of an umbrella repair man; a lean cat slunk across the cobbles and disappeared into a courtway; but for the most part the street was deserted save for the eccentric individual who had called forth my exclamation.

My friend rose lazily from the wicker rocker, in which he had been lounging, and came to my side, standing with long legs spread and hands in the pockets of his dressing gown. He smiled as he saw the singular personage coming along. A personage indeed he seemed to be, despite his odd actions, for he was tall and portly, with elderly whiskers of the brand known as mutton-chop, and he seemed eminently respectable. He was loping curiously, like a tired hound, lifting his knees high as he ran, and a heavy double watch chain of gold bounced against and rebounded from the plump line of his figured waistcoat. With one hand he clutched despairingly at his silk, two-gallon hat, while with the other he essayed weird gestures in the air in an emotion bordering upon distraction. We could almost see the spasmodic workings of his countenance.

"What under heaven can ail him?" I cried. "See how he glances at the houses as he passes."

"He is looking at the numbers," responded Sherlock Holmes, with dancing eyes, "and I fancy it is ours that will bring him the greatest happiness. His profession, of course, is obvious."

"A banker, I imagine, or at least a person of affluence," I hazarded, wondering what curious bit of minutiæ had betrayed the man's business to my remarkable companion, in a single glance.

"Affluent, yes," said Holmes, with a mischievous grin, "but not exactly a banker, Watson. Notice the sagging pockets, despite the excellence of his clothing, and the rather exaggerated madness of his eye. He is a collector, or I am very much mistaken."

"My dear fellow!" I exclaimed. "At his age and in his station! And why should he be seeking us? When we settled that last bill—"

"Of books," said my friend, severely. "He is a professional book collector. His line is Caxtons, Elzevirs, Gutenberg Bibles, folios; not the sordid reminders of unpaid grocery accounts and tobacconists' debits. See, he is turning in here, as I expected, and in a moment he will stand upon our hearthrug and tell us the harrowing tale of an unique volume and its extraordinary disappearance."

His eyes gleamed and he rubbed his hands together in profound satisfaction. I could not but hope that Holmes's conjecture was correct, for he had had little to occupy his mind for some weeks, and I lived in constant fear that he would seek that stimulation his active brain required in the long-tabooed cocaine bottle.

As Holmes finished speaking the man's ring at the doorbell echoed through the apartment;

hurried feet sounded upon the stairs, while the wailing voice of Mrs. Hudson, raised in agonized protest, could only have been occasioned by frustration of her coveted privilege of bearing his card to us. Then the door burst violently inward and the object of our analysis staggered to the center of the room and, without announcing his intention by word or sign, pitched head-foremost onto our center rug. There he lay, a magnificent ruin, with his head on the fringed border and his feet in the coal scuttle; and sealed within his lifeless lips the amazing story he had come to tell—for that it was amazing we could not doubt, in the light of our client's extraordinary behavior.

Holmes quickly ran for the brandy bottle, while I knelt beside the stricken mountain of flesh and loosened the wilted neckband. He was not dead, and, when we had forced the nozzle of the flask between his teeth, he sat up in groggy fashion, passing a dazed hand across his eyes. Then he scrambled to his feet with an embarrassed apology for his weakness, and fell into the chair which Holmes held invitingly toward him.

"That is right, Mr. Harrington Edwards," said my companion, soothingly. "Be quite calm, my dear Sir, and when you have recovered your composure you will find us ready to listen to your story."

"You know me then?" cried our sudden visitor, with pride in his voice and surprised eyebrows lifted.

"I had never heard of you until this moment, but if you wish to conceal your identity it would be well for you to leave your bookplates at home." As Holmes spoke he handed the other a little package of folded paper slips, which he had picked from the floor. "They fell from your hat when you had the misfortune to tumble," he added, with a whimsical smile.

"Yes, yes," cried the collector, a deep blush spreading over his features. "I remember now; my hat was a little large and I folded a number of them and placed them beneath the sweatband. I had forgotten."

"Rather shabby usage for a handsome etched plate," smiled my companion, "but that is your affair. And now, Sir, if you are quite at ease, let us hear what it is that has brought you, a collector of books, from Poke Stogis Manor—the name is on the plate—to the office of Mr. Sherlock Holmes, consulting expert in crime. Surely nothing but the theft of Mahomet's own copy of the Koran can have affected you so amazingly."

11

Mr. Harrington Edwards smiled feebly at the jest, then sighed. "Alas," he murmured, "if that were all it were! But I shall begin at the beginning.

"You must know, then, that I am the greatest Shakespearean commentator in the world. My collection of *ana* is unrivaled and much of the world's collection (and consequently its knowledge of the true Shakespeare) has emanated from my pen. One book I did not possess; it was unique, in the correct sense of that abused word; it was the greatest Shakespeare rarity in the world. Few knew that it existed, for its existence was kept a profound secret between a chosen few. Had it become known that this book was in England — any place, indeed — its owner would have been hounded to his grave by American millionaire collectors.

"It was in the possession of my friend — I tell you this in the strictest confidence, as between adviser and client — of my friend, Sir Nathaniel Brooke-Bannerman, whose place at Walton-on-Walton is next to my own. A scant two hundred yards separate our dwellings, and so intimate has been our friendship that a few years ago the fence between our estates was removed, and each roamed or loitered at will about the other's preserves.

12

"For some years, now, I have been at work on my greatest book—my *magnum opus*. It was to be also my last book, embodying the results of a lifetime of study and research. Sir, I know Elizabethan London better than any man alive, better than any man who ever lived, I sometimes think—" He burst suddenly into tears.

"There, there," said Sherlock Holmes, gently. "Do not be distressed. It is my business to help people who are unhappy by reason of great losses. Be assured, I shall help you. Pray continue with your interesting narrative. What was this book—which, I take it, in some manner has disappeared? You borrowed it from your friend?"

"That is what I am coming to," said Mr. Harrington Edwards, drying his tears, "but as for help, Mr. Holmes, I fear that is beyond even you. Yet, as a court of last resort, I came to you, ignoring all intermediate agencies.

"Let me resume then: As you surmise, I needed this book. Knowing its value, which could not be fixed, for the book is priceless, and knowing Sir Nathaniel's idolatry of it, I hesitated long before asking the loan of it. But I had to have it, for without it my work could not be completed, and at length I made the request.

I suggested that I go to his home, and go through the volume under his own eyes, he sitting at my side throughout my entire examination, and servants stationed at every door and window, with fowling pieces in their hands.

"You can imagine my astonishment when Sir Nathaniel laughed at my suggested precautions. 'My dear Edwards,' he said, 'that would be all very well were you Arthur Bambidge or Sir Homer Nantes (mentioning the two great men of the British Museum), or were you Mr. Henry Hutterson, the American railroad magnate; but you are my friend Edwards, and you shall take the book home with you for as long as you like.' I protested vigorously, I assure you, but he would have it so, and as I was touched by this mark of his esteem, at length I permitted him to have it his own way. My God! If I had remained adamant! If I had only—"

He broke off and for a moment stared fixedly into space. His eyes were directed at the Persian slipper on the wall, in the toe of which Holmes kept his tobacco, but we could see that his thoughts were far away.

"Come, Mr. Edwards," said Holmes, firmly. "You are agitating yourself unduly. And you are unreasonably prolonging our curiosity. You have not yet told us what this book is."

14

Mr. Harrington Edwards gripped the arm of the chair in which he sat, with tense fingers. Then he spoke, and his voice was low and thrilling:

"The book was a 'Hamlet' quarto, dated 1602, presented by Shakespeare to his friend Drayton, with an inscription four lines in length, written and signed by the Master, himself!"

"My dear sir!" I exclaimed. Holmes blew a long, slow whistle of astonishment.

"It is true," cried the collector. "That is the book I borrowed, and that is the book I lost! The long-sought quarto of 1602, actually inscribed in Shakespeare's own hand! His greatest drama, in an edition dated a year earlier than any that is known; a perfect copy, and with four lines in his handwriting! Unique! Extraordinary! Amazing! Astounding! Colossal! Incredible! Un—"

He seemed wound up to continue indefinitely, but Holmes, who had sat quite still at first, shocked by the importance of the loss, interrupted the flow of adjectives.

"I appreciate your emotion, Mr. Edwards," he said, "and the book is indeed all that you say it is. Indeed, it is so important that we must at once attack the problem of rediscovering it.

Compose yourself, my dear sir, and tell us of the loss. The book, I take it, is readily identifiable?"

"Mr. Holmes," said our client, earnestly, "it would be impossible to hide it. It is so important a volume that, upon coming into possession of it, Sir Nathaniel Brooke-Bannerman called a consultation of the great binders of the Empire, at which were present Mr. Riviere, Messrs. Sangorski & Sutcliffe, Mr. Zaehnsdorf and others. They and myself, and two others, alone know of the book's existence. When I tell you that it is bound in brown levant morocco, super extra, with leather joints, brown levant doublures and fly-leaves, the whole elaborately gold tooled, inlaid with 750 separate pieces of various colored leathers, and enriched by the insertion of eighty-two precious stones, I need not add that it is a design that never will be duplicated, and I tell you only a few of its glories. The binding was personally done by Messrs. Rivière, Sangorski, Sutcliffe, and Zaehnsdorf, working alternately, and is a work of such enchantment that any man might gladly die a thousand deaths for the privilege of owning it for five minutes."

"Dear me," quoth Sherlock Holmes, "it must indeed be a handsome volume, and from your description, together with a realization of its importance by reason of its association, I gather that it is something beyond what might be termed a valuable book.''

"Priceless!" cried Mr. Harrington Edwards. "The combined wealth of India, Mexico and Wall Street would be all too little for its purchase!"

"You are anxious to recover this book?" Holmes asked, looking at him keenly.

"My God!" shrieked the collector, rolling up his eyes and clawing the air with his hands. "Do you suppose—"

"Tut, tut!" Holmes interrupted. "I was only testing you. It is a book that might move even you, Mr. Harrington Edwards, to theft— but we may put aside that notion at once. Your emotion is too sincere, and besides you know too well the difficulties of hiding such a volume as you describe. Indeed, only a very daring man would purloin it and keep it long in his possession. Pray tell us how you came to suffer it to be lost."

Mr. Harrington Edwards seized the brandy flask, which stood at his elbow, and drained it at a gulp. With the renewed strength thus obtained, he continued his story:

"As I have said, Sir Nathaniel forced me to accept the loan of the book, much against my

17

own wishes. On the evening that I called for it, he told me that two of his trusted servants, heavily armed, would accompany me across the grounds to my home. 'There is no danger,' he said, 'but you will feel better,' and I heartily agreed with him. How shall I tell you what happened? Mr. Holmes, it was those very servants who assailed me and robbed me of my priceless borrowing!''

Sherlock Holmes rubbed his lean hands with satisfaction. "Splendid!" he murmured. "It is a case after my own heart. Watson, these are deep waters in which we are sailing. But you are rather lengthy about this, Mr. Edwards. Perhaps it will help matters if I ask you a few questions. By what road did you go to your home?''

"By the main road, a good highway which lies in front of our estates. I preferred it to the shadows of the wood.''

"And there were some 200 yards between your doors. At what point did the assault occur?''

"Almost midway between the two entrance drives, I should say.''

"There was no light?''

"That of the moon only.''

18

"Did you know these servants who accompanied you?"

"One I knew slightly; the other I had not seen before."

"Describe them to me, please."

"The man who is known to me, is called Miles. He is clean-shaven, short and powerful, although somewhat elderly. He was known, I believe, as Sir Nathaniel's most trusted servant; he had been with Sir Nathaniel for years. I cannot describe him minutely for, of course, I never paid much attention to him. The other was tall and thickset, and wore a heavy beard. He was a silent fellow; I do not believe he spoke a word during the journey."

"Miles was more communicative?"

"Oh yes — even garrulous, perhaps. He talked about the weather and the moon, and I forget what all."

"Never about books?"

"There was no mention of books between any of us."

"Just how did the attack occur?"

"It was very sudden. We had reached, as I say, about the halfway point, when the big man seized me by the throat — to prevent outcry, I suppose — and on the instant, Miles snatched the volume from my grasp and was off. In a moment his companion followed him. I had been half throttled and could not immediately cry out; when I could articulate, I made the countryside ring with my cries. I ran after them, but failed even to catch another sight of them. They had disappeared completely."

"Did you all leave the house together?"

"Miles and I left together; the second man joined us at the porter's lodge. He had been attending to some of his duties."

"And Sir Nathaniel—where was he?"

"He said good-night on the threshold."

"What has he had to say about all this?"

"I have not told him."

"You have not told him!" echoed Sherlock Holmes, in astonishment.

"I have not dared," miserably confessed our client. "It will kill him. That book was the breath of his life."

"When did this occur?" I put in, with a glance at Holmes.

"Excellent, Watson," said my friend, answering my glance. "I was about to ask the same question."

"Just last night," was Mr. Harrington Edwards' reply. "I was crazy most of the night; I didn't sleep a wink. I came to you the first thing this morning. Indeed, I tried to raise you on the telephone, last night, but could not establish a connection.''

"Yes," said Holmes, reminiscently, "we were attending Mme. Trontini's first night. You remember, Watson, we dined later at Albani's?"

"Oh, Mr. Holmes, do you think you can help me?" cried the abject collector.

"I trust so," declared my friend, cheerfully. "Indeed, I am certain that I can. At any rate, I shall make a gallant attempt, with Watson's aid. Such a book, as you remark, is not easily hidden. What say you, Watson, to a run down to Walton-on-Walton?"

"There is a train in half an hour," said Mr. Harrington Edwards, looking at his watch. "Will you return with me?"

"No, no," laughed Holmes, "that would never do. We must not be seen together just yet, Mr. Edwards. Go back yourself on the first train, by all means, unless you have further business in London. My friend and I will go together. There is another train this morning?"

"An hour later."

"Excellent. Until we meet, then!"

II

We took the train from Paddington Station an hour later, as we had promised, and began the journey to Walton-on-Walton, a pleasant, aristocratic village and the scene of the curious accident to our friend of Poke Stogis Manor. Holmes, lying back in his seat, blew earnest smoke rings at the ceiling of our compartment, which fortunately was empty, while I devoted myself to the morning paper. After a bit, I tired of this occupation and turned to Holmes. I was surprised to find him looking out of the window, wreathed in smiles and quoting Hafiz softly under his breath.

"You have a theory?" I asked, in surprise.

"It is a capital mistake to theorize in advance of the evidence," he replied. "Still, I have given some thought to the interesting problem of our friend, Mr. Harrington Edwards, and there are several indications which can point only to one conclusion."

"And whom do you believe to be the thief?"

"My dear fellow," said Sherlock Holmes, "you forget we already know the thief. Edwards has testified quite clearly that it was Miles who snatched the volume."

22

"True," I admitted, abashed. "I had forgotten. All we must do then, is find Miles."

"And a motive," added my friened, chuckling. "What would you say, Watson, was the motive in this case?"

"Jealousy," I replied promptly.

"You surprise me!"

"Miles had been bribed by a rival collector, who in some manner had learned about this remarkable volume. You remember Edwards told us this second man joined them at the lodge. That would give an excellent opportunity for the substitution of a man other than the servant intended by Sir Nathaniel. Is not that good reasoning?"

"You surpass yourself, my dear Watson," murmured Holmes. "It is excellently reasoned, and as you justly observe the opportunity for a substitution was perfect."

"Do you not agree with me?"

"Hardly, Watson. A rival collector, in order to accomplish this remarkable coup, first would have to have known of the volume, as you suggest, but also he must have known what night Mr. Harrington Edwards would go to Sir Nathaniel's to get it, which would point to collaboration on the part of our client. As a matter of fact, however, Mr. Edwards' decision as to his acceptance of the loan, was, I believe, sudden and without previous determination.''

''I do not recall his saying so.''

''He did not say so, but it is a simple deduction. A book collector is mad enough to begin with, Watson; but tempt him with some such bait as this Shakespeare quarto and he is bereft of all sanity. Mr. Edwards would not have been able to wait. It was just the night before that Sir Nathaniel promised him the book, and it was just last night that he flew to accept the offer — flying, incidentally, to disaster, also. The miracle is that he was able to wait for an entire day.''

''Wonderful!''

''Elementary,'' said Holmes. ''I have employed one of the earliest and best known principles of my craft, only. If you are interested in the process, you will do well to read Harley Graham on ''Transcendental Emotion,'' while I have, myself, been guilty of a small brochure in which I catalogue some twelve hundred professions, and the emotional effect upon their members of unusual tidings, good and bad.''

We were the only passengers to alight at Walton-on-Walton, but rapid inquiry developed that Mr. Harrington Edwards had returned on the previous train. Holmes, who had disguised himself before leaving the train, did all the talking. He wore his cap peak backwards, carried a pencil behind his ear and had turned up the bottoms of his trousers; from one pocket dangled the end of a linen tape measure. He was a municipal surveyor to the life, and I could not but think that, meeting him suddenly in the road, I should not myself have known him. At his suggestion, I dented the crown of my derby hat and turned my coat inside out. Then he gave me an end of the tape measure, while he, carrying the other end, went on ahead. In this fashion, stopping from time to time to kneel in the dust, and ostensibly to measure sections of the roadway, we proceeded toward Poke Stogis Manor. The occasional villagers whom we encountered on their way to the station bar-room, paid us no more attention than if we had been rabbits.

Shortly we came into sight of our friend's dwelling, a picturesque and rambling abode, sitting far back in its own grounds and bordered by a square of sentinel oaks. A gravel pathway led from the roadway to the house entrance, and, as we passed, the sunlight struck glancing rays from an antique brass knocker on the door. The whole picture, with its back-

25

ground of gleaming countryside, was one of rural calm and comfort; we could with difficulty believe it the scene of the sinister tragedy we were come to investigate.

"We shall not enter yet," said Sherlock Holmes, resolutely passing the gate leading into our client's acreage, "but we shall endeavor to be back in time for luncheon."

From this point the road progressed downward in a gentle incline and the trees were thicker on either side of the road. Holmes kept his eyes stolidly on the path before us, and when we had covered about one hundred yards he stopped. "Here," he said, pointing, "the assault occurred."

I looked closely at the earth, but could see no sign of struggle.

"You recall it was midway between the two houses that it happened," he continued. "No, there are few signs; there was no violent tussle. Fortunately, however, we had our proverbial fall of rain last evening and the earth has retained impressions nicely." He indicated the faint imprint of a foot, then another, and another. Kneeling down, I was able to see that, indeed, many feet had passed along the road.

Holmes flung himself at full length in the dirt and wriggled swiftly about, his nose to the earth, muttering rapidly in French. Then he whipped out a glass, the better to examine a mark that had caught his eye; but in a moment he shook his head in disappointment and continued with his examination. I was irresistibly reminded of a noble hound, at fault, sniffing in circles in an effort to reëstablish the lost scent. In a moment, however, he had it, for with a little cry of pleasure he rose to his feet, zigzagged curiously across the road and paused before a hedge, a lean finger pointing accusingly at a break in the thicket.

"No wonder they disappeared," he smiled as I came up. "Edwards thought they continued up the road, but here is where they broke through." Then stepping back a little distance, he ran forward lightly and cleared the hedge at a bound, alighting on his hands on the other side.

"Follow me carefully," he warned, "for we must not allow our own footprints to confuse us." I fell more heavily than my companion, but in a moment he had me by the heels and had helped me to steady myself. "See," he cried, lowering his face to the earth; and deep in the mud and grass I saw the prints of two pairs of feet.

"The small man broke through," said Holmes, exultantly, "but the larger rascal leaped over the hedge. See how deeply his prints are marked; he landed heavily here in the soft ooze. It is very significant, Watson, that they came this way. Does it suggest nothing to you?"

"That they were men who knew Edwards' grounds as well as the Brooke-Bannerman estate," I answered, and thrilled with pleasure at my friend's nod of approbation.

He lowered himself to his stomach, without further conversation, and for some moments we crawled painfully across the grass. Then a shocking thought came to me.

"Holmes," I whispered in horror, "do you see where these footprints tend? They are directed toward the home of our client, Mr. Harrington Edwards!"

He nodded his head slowly, and his lips were set tight and thin. The double line of impressions ended abruptly at the back door of Poke Stogis Manor!

Sherlock Holmes rose to his feet and looked at his watch.

"We are just in time for luncheon," he announced, and hastily brushed his garments. Then, deliberately, he knocked on the door. In a few moments we were in the presence of our client.

"We have been roaming about the neighborhood," apologized Holmes, "and took the liberty of coming to your rear entrance."

"You have a clew?" asked Mr. Harrington Edwards, eagerly.

A queer smile of triumph sat upon Sherlock Holmes' lips.

"Indeed," he said, quietly, "I believe I have solved your little problem, Mr. Harrington Edwards!"

"My dear Holmes!" I cried, and "My dear Sir!" cried our client.

"I have yet to establish a motive," confessed my friend, "but as to the main facts there can be no question."

Mr. Harrington Edwards fell into a chair, white and shaking.

"The book," he croaked. "Tell me!"

"Patience, my good sir," counseled Holmes, kindly. "We have had nothing to eat since sun-up, and are famished. All in good time. Let us first dine and then all shall be made clear. Meanwhile, I should like to telephone to Sir Nathaniel Brooke-Bannerman, for I wish him to hear what I have to say."

Our client's pleas were in vain. Holmes would have his little joke and his luncheon. In the end, Mr. Harrington Edwards staggered away to the kitchen to order a repast, and Sherlock Holmes talked rapidly and unintelligibly into the telephone for a moment and came back with a smile on his face, which, to me, boded ill for someone. But I asked no questions; in good time this amazing man would tell his story in his own way. I had heard all he had heard, and had seen all he had seen; yet I was completely at sea. Still, our host's ghastly smile hung in my mind, and come what would I felt sorry for him. In a little time we were seated at table. Our client, haggard and nervous, ate slowly and with apparent discomfort; his eyes were never long absent from Holmes' inscrutable face. I was little better off, but Holmes ate with gusto, relating meanwhile a number of his earlier adventures, which I may some day give to the world, if I am able to read my illegible notes made on the occasion.

When the sorry meal had been concluded, we went into the library, where Sherlock Holmes took possession of the big easy chair, with an air of proprietorship which would have been amusing in other circumstances. He screwed together his long pipe and lighted it with a malicious lack of haste, while Mr. Harrington Edwards perspired against the mantel in an agony of apprehension.

"Why must you keep us waiting, Mr. Holmes?" he whispered. "Tell us, at once, please, who—who—" His voice trailed off into a moan.

"The criminal," said Sherlock Holmes, smoothly, "is—"

"Sir Nathaniel Brooke-Bannerman!" said a maid, suddenly, putting her head in at the door, and on the heels of her announcement stalked the handsome baronet, whose priceless volume had caused all this stir and unhappiness.

Sir Nathaniel was white, and appeared ill. He burst at once into talk.

"I have been much upset by your call," he said, looking meanwhile at our client. "You say you have something to tell me about the quarto. Don't say—that—anything has happened—to it!" He clutched nervously at the wall to steady himself, and I felt deep pity for him.

Mr. Harrington Edwards looked at Sherlock Holmes. "Oh, Mr. Holmes," he cried, pathetically, "why did you send for him?"

"Because," said my friend, firmly, "I wish him to hear the truth about the Shakespeare quarto. Sir Nathaniel, I believe you have not been told as yet that Mr. Edwards was robbed, last night, of your precious volume—robbed by

31

the trusted servants whom you sent with him to protect it."

"What!" shrieked the titled collector. He staggered and fumbled madly at his heart; then collapsed into a chair. "Good God!" he muttered, and then again: "Good God!"

"I should have thought you would have been suspicious of evil when your servants did not return," pursued Holmes.

"I have not seen them," whispered Sir Nathaniel. "I do not mingle with my servants. I did not know they had failed to return. Tell me — tell me all!"

"Mr. Edwards," said Sherlock Holmes, turning to our client, "will you repeat your story, please?"

Mr. Harrington Edwards, thus adjured, told the unhappy tale again, ending with a heartbroken cry of "Oh, Sir Nathaniel, can you ever forgive me?"

"I do not know that it was entirely your fault," observed Holmes, cheerfully. "Sir Nathaniel's own servants are the guilty ones, and surely he sent them with you."

"But you said you had solved the case, Mr. Holmes," cried our client, in a frenzy of despair.

"Yes," agreed Holmes, "it is solved. You

have had the clue in your own hands ever since the occurrence, but you did not know how to use it. It all turns upon the curious actions of the taller servant, prior to the assault."

"The actions of —" stammered Mr. Harrington Edwards. "Why, he did nothing — said nothing!"

"That is the curious circumstance," said Sherlock Holmes, meaningly.

Sir Nathaniel got to his feet with difficulty.

"Mr. Holmes," he said, "this has upset me more than I can tell you. Spare no pains to recover the book, and to bring to justice the scoundrels who stole it. But I must go away and think — think —"

"Stay," said my friend. "I have already caught one of them."

"What! Where?" cried the two collectors, together.

"Here," said Sherlock Holmes, and stepping forward he laid a hand on the baronet's shoulder. "You, Sir Nathaniel, were the taller servant; you were one of the thieves who throttled Mr. Harrington Edwards and took from him your own book. And now, Sir, will you tell us why you did it?"

Sir Nathaniel Brooke-Bannerman toppled and would have fallen had not I rushed forward and supported him. I placed him in a chair. As we looked at him, we saw confession in his eyes; guilt was written in his haggard face.

"Come, come," said Holmes, impatiently. "Or will it make it easier for you if I tell the story as it occurred? Let it be so, then. You parted with Mr. Harrington Edwards on your doorsill, Sir Nathaniel, bidding your best friend good-night with a smile on your lips and evil in your heart. And as soon as you had closed the door, you slipped into an enveloping raincoat, turned up your collar and hastened by a shorter road to the porter's lodge, where you joined Mr. Edwards and Miles as one of your own servants. You spoke no word at any time, because you feared to speak. You were afraid Mr. Edwards would recognize your voice, while your beard, hastily assumed, protected your face, and in the darkness your figure passed unnoticed.

"Having choked and robbed your best friend, then, of your own book, you and your scoundrelly assistant fled across Mr. Edwards' fields to his own back door, thinking that, if investigation followed, I would be called in, and would trace those footprints and fix the crime upon Mr. Harrington Edwards, as part of a criminal plan, prearranged with your rascally servants, who would be supposed to be in the pay of Mr.

Edwards and the ringleaders in a counterfeit assault upon his person. Your mistake, Sir, was in ending your trail abruptly at Mr. Edwards' back door. Had you left another trail, then, leading back to your own domicile, I should unhesitatingly have arrested Mr. Harrington Edwards for the theft.

"Surely, you must know that in criminal cases handled by me, it is never the obvious solution that is the correct one. The mere fact that the finger of suspicion is made to point at a certain individual is sufficient to absolve that individual from guilt. Had you read the little works of my friend and colleague, here, Dr. Watson, you would not have made such a mistake. Yet you claim to be a bookman!"

A low moan from the unhappy baronet was his only answer.

"To continue, however: there at Mr. Edwards' own back door you ended your trail, entering his house—his own house—and spending the night under his roof, while his cries and ravings over his loss filled the night, and brought joy to your unspeakable soul. And in the morning, when he had gone forth to consult me, you quietly left—you and Miles—and returned to your own place by the beaten highway."

35

"Mercy!" cried the defeated wretch, cowering in his chair. "If it is made public, I am ruined. I was driven to it. I could not let Mr. Edwards examine the book, for exposure would follow, that way; yet I could not refuse him — my best friend — when he asked its loan."

"Your words tell me all that I did not know," said Sherlock Holmes, sternly. "The motive now is only too plain. The work, Sir, was a forgery, and knowing that your erudite friend would discover it, you chose to blacken his name to save your own. Was the book insured?"

"Insured for £350,000, he told me," interrupted Mr. Harrington Edwards, excitedly.

"So that he planned at once to dispose of this dangerous and dubious item, and to reap a golden reward," commented Holmes. "Come, Sir, tell us about it. How much of it was forgery? Merely the inscription?"

"I will tell you," said the baronet, suddenly, "and throw myself upon the mercy of my friend, Mr. Edwards. The whole book, in effect, was a forgery. It was originally made up of two imperfect copies of the 1604 quarto. Out of the pair, I made one perfect volume, and a skillful workman, now dead, changed the date for me so cleverly that only an expert of the first water could have detected it. Such an ex-

pert, however, is Mr. Harrington Edwards—
the one man in the world who could have un-
masked me."

"Thank you, Nathaniel," said Mr. Harrington Edwards, gratefully.

"The inscription, of course, also was
forged," continued the baronet. "You may as
well know all."

"And the book?" asked Holmes. "Where
did you destroy it?"

A grim smile settled on Sir Nathaniel's
features. "It is even now burning in Mr. Edwards' own furnace," he said.

"Then it cannot yet be consumed," cried
Holmes, and dashed into the basement. He was
absent for some little time, and we heard the
clinking of bottles, and, finally, the clang of a
great metal door. He emerged, some moments
later, in high spirits, carrying a charred leaf in
his hand.

"It is a pity," he cried, "a pity! In spite of
its questionable authenticity, it was a noble
specimen. It is only half consumed, but let it
burn away. I have preserved one leaf as a sou-
venir of the occasion." He folded it carefully
and placed it in his wallet. "Mr. Harrington
Edwards, I fancy the decision in this matter is
for you to announce. Sir Nathaniel, of course,

must make no effort to collect the insurance.''

"I promise that," said the baronet, quickly.

"Let us forget it, then," said Mr. Edwards, with a sigh. "Let it be a sealed chapter in the history of bibliomania." He looked at Sir Nathaniel Brooke-Bannerman for a long moment, then held out his hand. "I forgive you, Nathaniel," he said, simply.

Their hands met; tears stood in the baronet's eyes. Holmes and I turned from the affecting scene, powerfully moved. We crept to the door unnoticed. In a moment the free air was blowing on our temples, and we were coughing the dust of the library from our lungs.

III

"They are strange people, these book collectors," mused Sherlock Holmes, as we rattled back to town.

"My only regret is that I shall be unable to publish my notes on this interesting case," I responded.

"Wait a bit, my dear Doctor," advised Holmes, "and it will be possible. In time both of them will come to look upon it as a hugely diverting episode, and will tell it upon themselves. Then your notes will be brought forth

and the history of another of Mr. Sherlock
Holmes' little problems shall be given to the
world."

"It will always be a reflection upon Sir Nathaniel," I demurred.

"He will glory in it," prophesied Sherlock
Holmes. "He will go down in bookish chronicle
with Chatterton, and Ireland, and Payne Collier.
Mark my words, he is not blind even now to the
chance this gives him for sinister immortality.
He will be the first to tell it." (And so, indeed,
it proved, as this narrative suggests.)

"But why did you preserve the leaf from
Hamlet?" I curiously inquired. "Why not a
jewel from the binding?"

Sherlock Holmes chuckled heartily. Then he
slowly unfolded the page in question, and directed a humorous finger at a spot upon the page.

"A fancy," he responded, "to preserve so
accurate a characterization of either of our
friends. The line is a real jewel. See, the good
Polonius says: '*That he is mad, 'tis true: 'tis
true 'tis pittie; and pittie it is true.*' There is
as much sense in Master Will as in Hafiz or
Confucius, and a greater felicity of expres-
sion. . . Here is London, and now, my dear
Watson, if we hasten we shall be just in time for
Zabriski's matinee!"